5-Minute

Minute

MICKEY

Stories

Disney PRESS

Los Angeles • New York

Contents

Mickey's Perfecto Day!

Mickey and his pals are off to Madrid, Spain, and they have a *perfecto* day of sightseeing planned. "We're going to do it all, from the market at El Rastro to the square at Plaza Mayor!"

"Don't forget my concert with my friends the Three Caballeros," Donald reminds everyone.

"If we don't hurry, we'll never get there!" Goofy says.

On the road to Madrid, a baby bull named Francisco sits behind a gate, sniffing a red rose. Francisco loves roses.

When Mickey and the gang zoom past Francisco in their daily drivers, the rose flies off the bush. Mickey grabs it in midair and hands it to Minnie.

"Thank you, Mickey! It smells so pretty!" Minnie says. She tucks the rose behind her ear.

Francisco is startled to see his rose is gone! He pushes open the gate and gallops after it.

When the gang arrives in Madrid, Donald rushes off with Daisy to meet up with the rest of the band. "Come on, let's go meet Panchito and José!"

Mickey and Minnie start their *perfecto* day at El Rastro marketplace. They don't notice Francisco trotting along behind them, sniffing for his lost rose.

Minnie admires all the clothing, jewelry, and antiques. "Oh, Mickey, I could spend all day here," she squeals.

Mickey is pleased. Their perfectly planned *perfecto* day is going perfectly. As Minnie looks at dresses, Francisco peeks out and sniffs the rose behind Minnie's ear. He lets out a happy sigh.

"Minnie! There's a b-b-b-b-b-b-b-b—" Mickey stammers.

"A blouse? Belt? Bangle? Babushka?" Minnie guesses.

"Bull!" Mickey yells.

Mickey grabs Minnie's hand, and they take a running

leap into an empty cart.

Not too far away, Daisy and Donald arrive at Barrio de La Latina.
Donald spots José and Panchito having lunch at a café. "*Qué pasa*,
guys?" he greets them. "What's happening?"

"Hola, Don Donald!" Panchito replies. "It's good to see you, my
friend."

José asks, "Who is this charming señorita?"

Donald introduces Daisy. "I'm a huge fan," she says excitedly. "I
know all your songs!"

José notices Donald hungrily eyeing his plate of *patatas bravas*, a potato dish in a spicy sauce, and offers him some.

"Careful, those are really spicy," Panchito warns him.

It's too late. Donald has already taken a huge bite!

"Oh, dear!" Daisy cries. She hands Donald a glass of water. He gulps it down, and steam shoots from his ears.

Panchito plops a sombrero on Donald's head. "Now that you are warmed up, let's warm up."

They start to sing, but all Donald can do is wheeze.

"He lost his voice because of the spicy food!" Daisy says.

José says worriedly, "Unless his voice returns, someone else will have to sing his part at the concert!"

"But who could do that?" Daisy wonders aloud.

Panchito and José look at Daisy. "*You*, amiga!"

"Me?" Daisy says in surprise. "But Donald had his heart set on singing tonight."

Donald reluctantly puts his sombrero on Daisy's head.

To make Donald feel better, José orders him dessert. "Flan! It will make you feel like *el toro*—strong as a bull!"

Meanwhile, Mickey and Minnie are exploring the archways at the Puerta de Alcalá. Just when they think they have finally gotten rid of that pesky little bull, Francisco catches up to them. Mickey grabs Minnie by the hand, and the two of them race in and out of the arches with Francisco on their heels.

Then Mickey gets an idea.

When Francisco rounds a corner, Mickey and Minnie are gone!

"Um, Mickey, how did we get up here?" Minnie asks.

"By breaking the law . . . of *gravity*!" Mickey says.

Moments later they tumble to the ground with a thud. When Francisco sees them, Mickey and Minnie run off!

"I think we lost that bull!" Mickey says a few minutes later, relieved.

"And look!" Minnie points to Barrio de La Latina. "We're just in time for the concert."

José, Panchito, and Daisy take the stage and start to sing "Amigos Forever."

Donald sadly watches the concert from his table. When the waiter hands him the bill, Donald is furious about the price. *"WHAAAAT?"* Then he grins ear to ear. "My voice is back! José was right. The flan must have worked!"

Donald races up to the stage and joins Panchito, José, and Daisy in another round of "Amigos Forever."

The Four Caballeros are a huge hit! Mickey and Minnie are enjoying the show until . . .

Mickey leaps up. "Minnie! The bull is back!"

When Minnie sees that Francisco is focused on the rose, she smiles. "So that's why he's been after us! He just likes my flower, Mickey." She hands Francisco the rose, and he nuzzles her shoulder. "Awwww!"

Minnie leans over to give Mickey a peck on the cheek, but before she can, Francisco gives Mickey a thank-you for the flower!

Mickey giggles. "He's a sweet little fella, after all."
It is the perfect end to a *perfecto* day.

Minnie-rella

Today Mickey and his friends are planning a special surprise for a very special friend: Minnie!

"We've gotta keep Minnie busy until we get back with her present," Mickey tells them.

Just then, Minnie walks through the Clubhouse door.

"Say, would you mind doing us a few favors?" Goofy asks her.

Everyone hands Minnie something to clean or fix.

"Thanks, Minnie! See you later," Mickey says as he and the rest of the gang leave.

After a while, Minnie is so tired from
all the hard work that she drifts off
to sleep.

"Oh, Minnie-rella!" someone
calls.

"Oh, my! Who are you?"
Minnie-rella asks.

"I'm your fairy godmother!"
Clarabelle replies. "You should be
getting ready for Prince Mickey's ball."

"But I have too much to do and nothing
to wear," Minnie-rella says. "I wish I could go."

"I can make your wishes come true with my magic wand and some
Quoodles tools," says the Fairy Godmother.

And with that, Quoodles flies in with a pillow, Hilda the Hippo, a pink ribbon, and a mystery tool for later. But none of those things will help Minnie-rella clean the Clubhouse. Suddenly, she gets an idea. "Why didn't I think of it before? Oh, Handy Helpers!" Minnie-rella calls. The Clubhouse Handy Helpers help Minnie-rella and the Fairy Godmother sweep, dust, and scrub.

"Now you can go to the ball," the Fairy Godmother says.

"I don't think I can go wearing this," Minnie-rella replies.

The Fairy Godmother waves her wand . . . and a pile of fabric appears. "Gracious, that didn't work," she says.

The Fairy Godmother calls for help. Animal friends put Minnie-rella's dress together, and Quoodles brings ribbon for a new bow. *"Moo-la-la!"* the Fairy Godmother says.

"I think you're ready," says the Fairy Godmother. "Oh—except for those shoes! They won't do at all."

It takes her a few tries, but the Fairy Godmother makes sparkling glass slippers appear on Minnie-rella's feet.

"They're perfect!" Minnie-rella cries.

"*Now* you're ready!" the Fairy Godmother says.

"But how will I get
there?" Minnie-rella asks.

The Fairy
Godmother takes
Minnie-rella to
Goofy's garden for a
pumpkin.

"Pumpkins are out of
season," Goofy tells them.
"But I've got some lovely tomatoes."

"With a wave of my stick, this should do the trick!" the Fairy Godmother says. The tomato grows into a beautiful red-and-gold carriage. Goofy agrees to be the coachman.

"At twelve o'clock, the spell will be broken," the Fairy Godmother tells Minnie-rella, "and everything will turn back to what it was. You have to leave the ball by midnight."

As Minnie-rella and
Goofy are riding along,
they stop suddenly when
they drive over a hole
in the cobblestone
road. Minnie-rella calls
Quoodles and chooses
Hilda the Hippo. Hilda
gives the carriage a firm
kick, sending it rolling
down the road.

"Thank you, Hilda!" Minnie-rella calls.
Hilda gives her a "you're welcome" curtsy.

A bit farther along, Goofy drops off Minnie-rella at the castle gate. "To open the gate, you need three diamond shapes," Royal Gatekeeper Pete tells them.

Minnie-rella calls for Quoodles. She picks the mystery tool: it's a charm bracelet. Minnie-rella gives Pete three diamond charms. He unlocks the gate and sends her on her way.

Minnie-rella's wish has come true at last!

A trumpet blares. "Hear ye, hear ye," Professor Von Drake announces. "His royal highness, Prince Mickey, and his royal pooch, Pluto!"

Prince Mickey walks over to Minnie-rella and asks her to dance. They spin and twirl across the dance floor all night.

Suddenly, the clock begins to strike twelve. "Oh, no!" Minnie-rella cries. "I have to go!"

"Wait!" Prince Mickey calls after her. "I don't even know your name."

But Minnie-rella doesn't stop running, not even when one of her glass slippers falls off.

Prince Mickey can't believe his princess ran away. "How will I ever find her?" he says sadly.

Pluto sniffs his way over to the lost shoe. "It's a clue!" says the professor. "As your royal adviser, I advise you to find the one who fits the glass slipper."

Prince Mickey starts right away. But first he finds Goofy, who greets him with a deep bow. "May I be of service?"

Prince Mickey tells Goofy about the runaway princess and the glass slipper. "Everybody in the land has got to try it on and see if it fits."

"Okey dokey!" Goofy says, grabbing the shoe. He squeezes it onto his foot, but it pops off and goes flying!

Quoodles arrives with the pillow just in time for Prince Mickey to catch the slipper before it hits the ground.

"*Gawrsh*, that glass slipper sure does look familiar," says Goofy. "Now, where do I think I remember seeing it?"

Back at the Clubhouse, Minnie-rella is telling her animal friends every detail of her incredible evening at the castle when, all of a sudden, there is a knock at the door.

Prince Mickey walks in holding the glass slipper. "I believe you lost this," he says, and places it on Minnie-rella's foot. It fits perfectly!

Just then, the Fairy Godmother appears. With a wave of her wand, Minnie-rella is wearing her ballgown, tiara, and both glass slippers once again. "Prince Mickey and Princess Minnie-rella, you will live happily ever after!"

"Wake up, Minnie!" Mickey calls.

Minnie sits up and stretches. "Oh, hello, everybody," she says. "I must have fallen asleep."

"We have a special surprise for you because you're such a great friend," Mickey tells her.

Minnie gasps when she opens the box. "Thank you! I've dreamed of wearing shoes like these."

"You look as pretty as a princess," Mickey tells her.

Minnie smiles back at him. "Oh, Mickey, you'll always be my prince."

The friends do the Hot Dog Dance.

Minnie loves her new glass slippers.

She does the best dance of all!

Super Adventure

"Hiya, everybody," says Mickey. "Welcome to the Clubhouse!"

Today Mickey and his pals are pretending to be superheroes.

"Superheroes work together to save the day from supervillains," Mickey explains.

Donald pretends to be the bad guy. "You'll never defeat me!" he shouts.

The superheroes chase Donald every which way.

"Wait! We're supposed to work as a super-team," Mickey says. But the heroes don't listen and end up in a jumble on the ground.

Just then, a shadow falls over the gang.

"Gawrsh!" says Goofy. "It's a giant hot-dog balloon."

"That's a zeppelin," says Mickey. "But what's it doing here?"

Suddenly, the zeppelin zaps the Glove Balloon with a shrink ray!

Power-Pants Pete flies down. "Stay back," he warns. "I'm about to shrink everything in the Clubhouse World!"

Power-Pants Pete picks up the tiny Glove Balloon and flies off!

"We have to stop Pete from shrinking everything!" says Mickey.

Goofy scratches his head. "This is a super-problem," he says.

"Did someone say 'super'?" asks Professor Von Drake. "I have just the thingamajig you need!"

The professor has a new invention.

"I call it the Super-Maker Machine," he says.

"It makes soup?" asks Goofy.

"No, Goofy," laughs the professor. "It will make real superheroes out of all of you."

"Super cheers," says Mickey. "That's just what we need!"

"Then step right in," the professor says.

"Now you all have super-fantastic powers!" the professor exclaims. "But you'll have to work together to stop Power-Pants Pete."

"Don't worry," says Super Mickey. "The Clubhouse Heroes are on the job!"

"One more thing," the professor adds. "You'll only have your powers for a little while. When your Superpower Bands turn red, your powers will go kaput."

"Then we'd better get going!" says Minnie.

Power-Pants Pete is about to shrink Minnie's Bow-tique!

Upsy-Daisy uses her mind powers.

Wonder Minnie throws her Super-Wonder Bows.

But nothing works.

"Your powers blocked each other," says Mickey.

Suddenly, Pete drops hundreds of rubber duckies!

Mickey calls for help. "Oh, Super Toodles!"

Super Toodles has four Super Mouseketools: a giant blow-dryer, a catcher's mitt, a big umbrella, and a Mystery Mouseketool.

The big umbrella does the trick. The rubber duckies bounce right off.

But Pete shrinks Minnie's Bow-tique anyway and zooms off!

Pete's next target is the Eiffel Tower.

The heroes have to hurry. Their Superpower Bands are turning red! Super Goof and Dynamo Duck get all twisted and hit the zeppelin. Pete falls to the ground!

"You're through, Power-Pants Pete!" says Super Mickey.

"I'm sorry," says Pete. "But the big boss made me do it!"

The zeppelin lands, and out comes the big boss: Megamort!

"It's shrinking time," he says. Megamort makes Pete tiny with his shrink ray.

"Oh, that tickled," says Pete.

"You're just a mean ol' meany villain," says Minnie.

"I'm taking the Clubhouse World for myself!" Megamort says as he jumps in the zeppelin and takes off again.

"We have to catch Megamort," says Mickey. "Our powers are almost gone!" Mickey and Superpower Pup zoom into the sky and grab hold of the zeppelin. But Megamort traps them in a superstrong bubble!

"We need a Mouseketool," says Mickey. "Oh, Super Toodles!"

Mickey chooses the giant blow-dryer. It works! The blow-dryer blows all the bubbles away. "Bye-bye, bubbles!" says Mickey.

Back on the ground, Tiny Pete is rolling down a hill!

"We've got to catch Pete before it's too late," Super Goof says.

Dynamo Duck runs out ahead of his friends. "I'm on the job!" he calls—but he is not watching where he's going and falls. The heroes trip over each other and land in a heap.

"Tiny Pete is rolling away, and our Superpower Bands are all red!" says Daisy.

In a flash, the Clubhouse Heroes lose all their superpowers!

Up in the zeppelin, Megamort takes aim at the Clubhouse. Mickey tries to stop him, but he loses his powers, too.

As Mickey falls toward the ground, Megamort zaps him and the Clubhouse! Megamort scoops up Mickey and the Clubhouse and takes them up to the zeppelin.

Minnie and the rest of the heroes are still trying to save Tiny Pete.
"We have to catch him," shouts Minnie. "Oh, Super Toodles!"
Minnie chooses the catcher's mitt and tosses it to Goofy, who
makes the catch! "We did it!" says Minnie. "We worked together as a
team!"

All at once, the gang is turned back into superheroes!

"When we work together," says Minnie, "we're super-duper!" She looks up. "Uh-oh. Megamort has captured Mickey!"

"We gotta save him," says Goofy. "Oh, Super Toodles!"

The gang picks the Mystery Mouseketool. It's a superjet!

"Up and away," says Minnie. "Let's save the day!"

The heroes plan to work together to rescue Mickey.

Goofy and Donald sneak aboard the zeppelin and find the shrunken
Clubhouse World. They quickly gather up all the globes. Megamort
tries to stop them, but Tiny Mickey trips him up just in time!

The heroes bring the zeppelin to a sudden stop.

Goofy, Donald, and Mickey tumble out and land right in the superjet! But the zeppelin springs a leak and flies out of control. "Megamort needs help!" shouts Mickey.

"But he's a villain," says Goofy.

"He still needs saving," says Mickey. "And that's what heroes do!"

Pluto helps Wonder Minnie tie up the zeppelin with her Super-Wonder Bows. Everyone works together to pull the zeppelin to the ground.

"We did it!" they shout.

Megamort scrambles out of the flattened zeppelin.

"After all I did, I can't believe you rescued me," he says. "Thank you."

"You're welcome, Mr. Megamort," says Goofy.

"I'm really Mortimer Mouse," Megamort reveals. "I'm your new neighbor."

"Well, you weren't acting very neighborly," Minnie points out.

Mortimer agrees. He reverses the shrink ray and returns Mickey and Pete to their normal sizes!

Then Mortimer unshrinks the whole Clubhouse World.

"I'm sorry," he says. "I thought if I took what you had, I'd be happy."

"The Clubhouse is all about having friends," says Mickey.

"That's just it," Mortimer admits. "I don't have any friends."

"You do now!" says Goofy.

"That's super!" Mortimer says.

"It's more than super," says Mickey. "It's super-duper!"

Farmer Donald's Pumpkin Patch

"Look at this!" says Daisy as she walks into the Clubhouse one day. "This pumpkin won the grand prize at the County Fair!"

"Hot dog!" says Mickey. "That is one big pumpkin!"

Donald takes a look at the picture. "Aw, phooey!" he says. "I could grow a garden filled with the biggest pumpkins you've ever seen! I'm sure it's easy to do."

The next day, Donald decides to grow his own prize pumpkin. He throws a handful of pumpkin seeds in the dirt behind the Clubhouse.

"I think it takes more than that to grow a garden," says Minnie.

Mickey nods. "First you need to make holes in the dirt, put a seed in each hole, and then cover them up."

"That's a lot of work," says Donald. "I'm sure the seeds will be fine where they are."

"Maybe Toodles can help," says Mickey. "Oh, Toodles!"

Toodles flies in with three Mouseketools: a pogo stick, a mirror, and an elephant.

"Hmm," Donald says. "Which Mouseketool can help us make holes for the seeds?"

"I think it's this one," says Minnie as she points to the pogo stick.

Donald hops on the pogo stick and starts bouncing in the dirt. Minnie is right! The pogo stick makes holes that are just the right size.

Then Donald drops a few seeds into each hole and covers them all with dirt.

"See, I told you this would be easy," says Donald as he sits back down. "Now all we have to do is watch the seeds grow." Donald, thinking his work is done, closes his eyes to rest.

"I think it takes more than that to grow a garden," says Daisy.

"A garden needs water," Mickey says. "Water helps seeds grow."

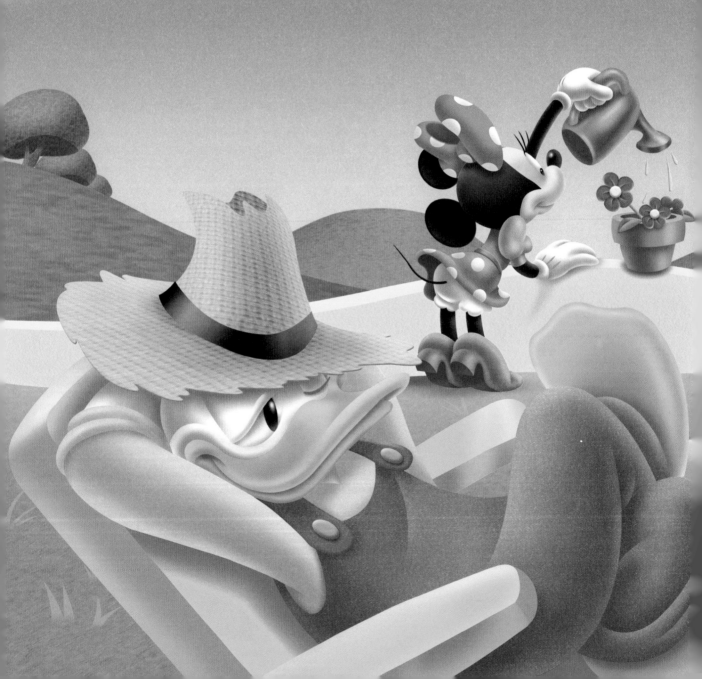

"Mickey's right," says Minnie.

"But how am I going to water this big garden?" asks Donald. "That's a lot of work. I'll just wait for it to rain."

"It's time to call Toodles again," says Mickey. "Oh, Toodles!"

"Let's pick the elephant," says Daisy, looking at the remaining tools. The elephant takes a big drink from the pond. Then, using her trunk, she sprinkles water over the entire garden. Daisy was right!

"I told you this would be easy," says Donald as he sits back down. "I'll have that trophy in no time."

"I think it takes more than that to grow a garden," says Mickey.

Donald looks puzzled. "But what else is there to do?"

"Plants need sun," says Minnie, "and your garden is in the shade."

"But we can't move the sun!" Donald squawks.

"Maybe we can," says Mickey. "Oh, Toodles!"

Toodles has just one tool left—a mirror.

"A mirror?" asks Donald. "How can that help my garden grow?"

Mickey and Minnie place the mirror so it reflects the sunlight onto the garden.

"Oh, boy!" shouts Donald. "Now we'll just watch the seeds grow."

Daisy giggles. "Today was just the beginning of your garden, Farmer Donald," she says. "Now you have to make sure the garden keeps getting plenty of water and sunlight and care every day!"

Donald is surprised at how much work it takes to grow a garden. But over the next few months, he takes care of his pumpkins every day, from seeds to sprouts to long, thick vines bursting with pumpkins. When it is time for the contest, Donald picks the biggest, brightest, most beautiful pumpkin from his garden, and then the whole gang heads to the fair.

Judge Goofy walks around and looks at all the pumpkins. Finally he says, "The prize for the biggest pumpkin goes to Farmer Donald!" Everyone cheers for their friend.

"Next year, I think I'll enter the apple-pie contest," says Daisy.

"Good idea!" Donald declares. "I'll plant a great big apple orchard so you'll have all the apples you need. I'm sure it's easy to do!"

One Unicorny Day

Penelope Pony is having a great day at the Longtree Horse Ranch. Lisa is busy tending to the other animals when Penelope spots a butterfly. Suddenly, Penelope is running out of the ranch.

Penelope chases the butterfly off the ranch, over a hill, and into Mickey's Garage. She gallops past Goofy, who is testing out his new cotton candy maker.

"Yummers!" says Goofy.

"Neigh!" whinnies Penelope.

Crash goes the cart. *Splat* goes the pretty pink cotton candy—right on Penelope's head!

Penelope follows the butterfly into Minnie's makeover salon.

Before she knows it, she is getting a makeover herself!

A bit of glitter here . . .

A little paint there . . .

Penelope gets made over mane to tail.

She looks like a pretty, sparkly, magical unicorn!

Penelope trots around, following the beautiful butterfly. She has never seen anything like it before. She chases it past Pluto's doghouse.

And then she just about catches the butterfly while she is running by Clarabelle's house. Clarabelle is shocked.

In her excitement, Clarabelle calls Daisy. "I just saw a unicorn on my street!"

Daisy gasps. "I love unicorns!" she exclaims. "I'll be right there!"

Daisy rushes over to her friends. "Clarabelle saw a unicorn run past her house!" she says.

"Phooey!" Donald huffs. "There's no such thing as unicorns." He crosses his arms and looks at Mickey. Mickey and Goofy both shrug.

"Just because you've never seen one doesn't mean they aren't real," Daisy tells Donald. She drives to Clarabelle's as fast as she can.

Just then, Mickey gets a phone call. It is Lisa from the Longtree Horse Ranch.

"Hi, Mickey. My pony Penelope wandered off. Could you help me round her up?"

"Sure thing," Mickey replies. "Saddle up, everybody!" Mickey tells the gang about the missing pony.

"Wait a minute," Minnie says to herself. "A missing pony *and* a unicorn sighting on the very same day?"

Daisy pulls up in front of Clarabelle's house. "Which way did it go?" Daisy asks.

Clarabelle points down the road, and Daisy zooms off right away.

Daisy drives until she sees a trail of glittery horseshoe prints. "The unicorn can't be far!" she squeals.

Daisy is excited. She follows the trail of horseshoes as far as she can.

Meanwhile, Donald is driving downtown when he spots a pony. He twirls his lasso and ropes it.

"Gotcha, Penelope!" he shouts. He pulls on his rope and stops his car just beside the horse. He is very proud of himself for being the one to wrangle the pony.

But when Donald finally catches up with the pony, he sees that it isn't Penelope after all. It is just two people dressed up as a pony for a costume party.

Donald is furious and begins yelling at the two partygoers. And he is wondering where Penelope can be and if he is ever going to find her.

Just then, Penelope trots past them. She is still following the butterfly. Donald's jaw drops to the ground.

"The unicorn is real?" Donald sputters. "I can't believe it . . . but I saw it with my own two eyes!"

Donald sees Minnie drive by. He waves her down. "Minnie! I just saw the unicorn!" he shouts.

"Are you sure?" Minnie asks.

"I'm sure! I'm sure," Donald replies. "Look! There's unicorn dust on my bumper."

Minnie takes a closer look and giggles. "Donald, that's not unicorn dust," she says. "It's paint from my makeover salon. I'd recognize it anywhere!"

Not far away, as Daisy drives past the park, she sees something glittery and sparkly in the sunlight. "The unicorn's over there!" she cries.

Daisy speeds over to where she saw the unicorn. Carefully, she goes to investigate what is in the bushes. She is sure to move slowly so she won't spook the unicorn. After all, Daisy has spent all this time looking for it. She doesn't want it running away.

Mickey, Minnie, Donald, and Goofy arrive just in time to see Penelope step out from the bushes.

"Hot dog!" Mickey shouts. "The unicorn is real!"

"Gawrsh!" Goofy guffaws. "A unicorny!"

Goofy accidentally bumps his head against the Tubster's plumbing. Water blasts from the showerhead, and Penelope prances into the spray.

"The unicorn is a . . . pony?" Daisy says in disbelief.

"I'm sorry, Daisy," Minnie says. "Penelope wandered off the ranch and got into my makeover salon. She must have gotten spray-painted, and everyone thought she was a unicorn."

"Well, she might not be real, but that doesn't mean there aren't real unicorns out there somewhere!" Daisy insists.

Lisa comes to pick up Penelope and take her back to the ranch. She thanks everyone for their help in finding Penelope. "I hope she didn't cause too much trouble today," Lisa says.

The friends wave goodbye to Lisa and Penelope.

As Lisa and Penelope Pony drive away, Daisy is distracted by
something on a hill just through the park. She points and gets very
excited. Donald looks at what she is pointing at and shakes his head.
"Magical!" Daisy says with a happy sigh. "I knew they were real!"

Race for the Rigatoni Ribbon

Mickey and his pals are getting their daily drivers tuned up and ready for the biggest race of the year in Rome, Italy: the Race for the Rigatoni Ribbon. Mickey and Donald are having a friendly argument over which one of them will win.

"Gawrsh," Goofy says. "Doesn't that fancy feller Piston Pietro win every year?"

"Not this year," says Minnie. She and Daisy are already planning the perfect outfits to go with the Rigatoni Ribbon when *they* win.

Race day has finally arrived! The racers zoom up to the starting line. Suddenly, Piston Pietro roars up in his Super Crusher. "You can't start without today's winner—me!" he says. "You losers can't win anything driving those little toy cars!"

But the gang's daily drivers are no ordinary cars.

With a grin and a wink, Mickey calls out, "Let's show Pietro what we can do!"

Minnie agrees. "Bow-tastic idea, Mickey!"

One by one, each of the racers presses a button on the dashboard.

WHOOSH! POP! BANG! Pietro can't believe his eyes as the daily drivers transform into supercool roadsters!

"On your marks, get set . . ." Clarabelle shouts. "Get *mooooooo*-ving!"

The racers zoom off!

Pietro zigzags across the racetrack and takes the lead—and to stay there, he has a few tricks up his sleeve. "Time for the Pizza Pie Flip-and-Fly." Pietro snickers as he pulls a lever.

Pietro's roadster starts shooting out pizzas! Mickey swerves. "Hey, no fair!" he calls.

"Who cares about fair?" Pietro shouts. "I do whatever it takes to win!"

Poor Goofy is positively pummeled with pizzas. His roadster spins off down the wrong street.

Goofy's roadster comes to a stop in front of a restaurant. "Look at
the size of that meatball!" he says. "I gotta get me a taste." He runs in
and orders spaghetti and meatballs with extra pepper. "Yummers!"

All the pepper makes Goofy sneeze! *ACHOOOOO!*

His forks fly out of his hands and hit the giant meatball, causing it to
roll down the street! But Goofy just grabs two new forks and digs in.

Back on the racetrack, Minnie and Daisy are catching up to Pietro. "They are too close for comfort," Pietro says to himself. "Time to give them the slip, Italian-style!" Pietro flips a switch and spills olive oil across the road, sending the girls spinning off the track!

"Oh, dear," Minnie says. "We're way off course!"

Suddenly, they drive past Floochi's, the most famous shoe store in Italy.

"Well," says Daisy, "we could make a pit stop. . . ."

Minnie agrees, as long as it's quick. They haven't forgotten about the Rigatoni Ribbon!

The race is down to three drivers. Pietro turns around to gloat at Mickey and Donald. That's when they all see something that does not belong on the racetrack!

"AHHHHH! A GIANT MEATBALL!" they scream.

Pietro wastes no time racing through the gate and slamming it shut behind him. Mickey and Donald could get flattened any second!

Mickey spots a long smooth stone that looks just like a ramp. "Donald, follow my lead!" he calls. Mickey roars up the ramp with Donald right behind him.

"Heads up!" Donald calls. "Here comes the duck!" He and Mickey rocket through the air and land safely on the racetrack.

"And here goes the mouse!" Mickey adds.

Pietro is furious. "Ooh, I'll show those rotten Roadster Racers!" he yells.

But this race is far from over! Minnie, Daisy, and Goofy are back from their pit stops and gaining speed. The Rigatoni Ribbon is still up for grabs!

Suddenly, the racers hear a rumbling: it's the giant meatball! It bounces down the road and lands with a splat, sending Goofy and Pietro flying.

Mickey turns around to see the massive meatball on the racetrack. But Donald is too focused on the finish line to notice.

Mickey realizes that Donald is about to be flattened! He throws his Hot Doggin' Hot Rod into reverse and races backward.

"You're going the wrong way!" Donald cries out.

"Forget about me," Mickey says. "Go win the race!" Mickey roars his roadster into the meatball, sending it, Pietro, and Goofy flying sky-high.

Donald zooms across the finish line. "I did it! I beat Piston Pietro!" he cries.

With one last big bounce, the meatball lands on a statue and explodes into dozens of tiny meatballs that rain down from the sky. It's the perfect time for a plate of pasta!

Clarabelle puts the Rigatoni Ribbon around Donald's neck.

"Sorry you didn't win, pal—but I won thanks to you, Mickey!" Donald says.

"Aw," Mickey replies. "Friendship is a lot more important to me than winning."

Dr. Daisy, M.D.

CRASH! BANG! BOOM!

Oh, no! Goofy trips on his way into the Clubhouse.

"Are you all right, Goofy?" asks Mickey.

"I think so," Goofy replies. He touches his head, his arm, and his nose to make sure. "There's a boo-boo on my nose!" Goofy cries. "Gawrsh, I've got a boo-boo!"

Just then, Daisy walks into the Clubhouse. "Did someone say 'boo-boo'?" she asks. "I bet I can make Goofy feel better." Daisy disappears for a moment and returns wearing a white coat and doctor's mirror. She walks over to her friend and takes a good look at his swollen red nose. "Hmmm," she says, "it looks like Goofy's boo-boo just needs to cool down a bit."

"Great idea, Daisy!" says Mickey. "Let's blow some air onto Goofy's boo-boo."

It works! Goofy's boo-boo is all better.

"Wahoo, you did it!" Goofy says. "Thanks, Daisy."

"I want to be the best pretend doctor in the whole wide world," says Daisy. "And someday I want to get my pretend-doctor sticker!"

Mickey and Goofy want to help their friend get a special sticker. Mickey turns the Clubhouse into an office. Goofy finds four pretend patients: Pluto, Minnie, Donald, and a mystery patient.

Toodles arrives with Mouseketools for Daisy to help her patients with. He brings a giraffe, a piggy bank, a magnifying glass, and a Mystery Mouseketool.

Daisy is ready for her first patient. "Hello, Pluto," says Dr. Daisy. "What's the matter?"

Pluto holds up his paw, and Dr. Daisy sees the pretend thorn that is stuck in it.

Which one of the Mouseketools can help Dr. Daisy pull out the thorn? Can the giraffe help? No, that's silly! What about the piggy bank? No, that can't help either. The magnifying glass can help Daisy see the thorn but not pull it out. It's time to use the Mystery Mousketool—toy tweezers!

Using the toy tweezers, Dr. Daisy gently removes the pretend thorn from Pluto's paw. Pluto barks his thanks.

"Hot dog!" says Mickey. "We're ready to call the next patient!"

"Hi there, Minnie," says Dr. Daisy. "What's the matter?"

Minnie points to her stomach and says, "I have a tummy ache."

"I see," says Dr. Daisy. "Well, there's only one way to help a tummy ache. And that's with an apple, of course!"

"Oh, I know where we can get apples," says Mickey. "From an apple tree!"

"We're going to need a Mouseketool to reach them," says Daisy.

Which Mouseketool can help them reach the apples high up in a tall trcc? The giraffe!

But when the friends get to the apple tree,
the giraffe starts to eat all the apples!

Just before the giraffe can get the last one,
Mickey reaches up and grabs it. Then he tosses
the shiny green apple to Minnie.

Minnie feels better after just one bite. "Thank you,
Dr. Daisy . . . and Mickey!" she says with a giggle.

Back in the pretend doctor's office, it is time for the next patient.

"Well, it's about time!" says Donald as he marches into Dr. Daisy's office. He holds out his arms to the doctor. "They're asleep!"

"Hmm," says Dr. Daisy, "I think I can fix sleeping arms—with jumping beans! If you hold a jar of jumping beans in your hands, they'll shake your arms awake in no time."

"Jumping beans?" Donald squawks. "Where am I supposed to find those?"

"I know where we can get some," says Mickey. "But we'll need coins."

Which Mouseketool can give Mickey and Daisy coins? The piggy bank!

Mickey and Daisy
head to Clarabelle's
Moo Mart. A jar
of jumping beans
costs six coins. The
piggy bank has exactly
enough.

The jumping beans
work! Donald thanks
Dr. Daisy for fixing
his sleeping arms.

It is time for the last patient—the mystery patient. Who is wrapped in that big spotted blanket?

It's Pete!

"How can I help you, Pete?" Dr. Daisy asks.

Pete points to his spots. "I've got these spotty spots everywhere!" he says. "You'll never figure out what's wrong with me." He laughs.

"Gee," says Dr. Daisy, "I need to get a close look at those spots."
Which Mouseketool can help Dr. Daisy? The magnifying glass!

"Hey, we've used all our Mouseketools!" says Mickey. "Let's all say super cheers!"

Dr. Daisy sees a chicken inside each spot. Pete has pretend chicken pox.

"The only way to get rid of chicken pox is to shake the spots off with the chicken dance!" says Dr. Daisy. She, Mickey, and Pete start dancing right away.

"Dr. Daisy, you are a genius!" says Pete.

Dr. Daisy laughs. "Who? Me?" she says.

Dr. Daisy has finally earned her pretend-doctor sticker. She is so proud. "I couldn't have done it without your help," she says. "Thank you, everybody!"

"What a hot-dog day," says Mickey. "See you real soon!"

Minnie's Pet Salon

Today is the day of Pluto's All-Star Pet Show! All the Clubhouse pets will be onstage. But only one will win the prize for Best in Show!

Minnie will help get the pets ready. "Welcome to Minnie's Pet Salon," she says. "It's time for me to open for business!"

The friends bring their pets to the salon.

Goofy brings his kitty, Mr. Pettibone. "And my frog, Fiona, needs to get ready, too," he says.

Daisy drops off her bunny, Captain Jumps-a-Lot.

"Here's my adorable puppy, Bella," says Clarabelle.

Pete is right behind her. "I'm dropping off Butch!" he says.

Then Donald runs up. "Boo-Boo Chicken wants to come, too!"

So many pets! Minnie will need help from her friends to get them all ready in time for the show.

The first station
is the Dog and Cat
Wash. Daisy and
Pluto are ready to
give Bella a bath.
Daisy fills the tub
with warm water
and pours in the
bath soap.

Pink bubbles
grow and grow!

"Oh, no!" says Daisy. "There are too many bubbles." She jumps
into the tub to find Bella.

Minnie comes to the rescue. "We need a Mouseketool!" she says.

Toodles brings a
baby elephant.

She fills her trunk with water and rinses the bubbles away. "Yay!"
shouts Daisy. "Now Bella is ready for Pluto's pet show."

At the Beauty Bar, Donald is trying to put bows on Figaro and Mr. Pettibone, but they won't sit still!

Minnie brings Toodles over to help. Toodles has three Mouseketools left.

"Let's try the beach towel," Minnie says.

Donald holds
the beach towel,
and Figaro and
Mr. Pettibone
jump right in.

"What a *purr*-fect solution," says Minnie. Then she and Donald put bows on the kitties.

"Thanks for helping me, Minnie," says Donald.

Next Minnie goes to check on Mickey. He's trying to teach Captain Jumps-a-Lot and Fiona to jump together.

"Maybe they'll do it if we give them a beat," says Minnie.

Mickey and Minnie jump together and chant, "One, two, jump when we do. Three, four, jump once more."

It works! The bunny and frog hop at the same time.

"That was fun!" says Minnie.

Suddenly, Butch and Bella run past, pulling Goofy behind them.

"Slow down, doggies!" yells Goofy. "Whoa!"

"We've got to help Goofy—fast!" says Mickey. "Oh, Toodles!"

Mickey picks the Mystery Mouseketool. It's a big sock!

"Come here, doggies!" shouts Mickey. "Look what I have for you."
The dogs stop running and play with the sock.

As evening comes, it's time for the pet show to begin. Pete and Clarabelle will be the judges.

"May the best pet win!" says Clarabelle.

Goofy turns on the lights. But nothing happens!

"Gawrsh," says Goofy. "The lights aren't working."

"Oh, no," Minnie says sadly. "We can't put on the show without light."

Mickey knows just what to do.

"Oh, Toodles!" he calls once more. Toodles rushes to the stage. He has one more Mouseketool—a jar full of fireflies!

"Can the fireflies light up the paper lanterns?" asks Mickey.

Pluto barks and wags his tail.

"You betcha, Pluto," says Mickey. "Super cheers!"
The colorful lights are beautiful.
"Now it's time for Pluto's All-Star Pet Show!" Mickey calls.
"Woof-woof," barks Pluto.

Donald takes Boo-Boo Chicken to the stage.

He does a chicken dance!

Wonderful!

Next Butch and Bella twirl

and prance in costumes.

Delightful!

Minnie and Goofy

hold up hoops as Figaro and Mr. Pettibone do tricks.

Amazing!

Captain Jumps-a-Lot and
Fiona dazzle the audience
with their jumping trick.
Fantastic!

Clarabelle and Pete can't decide which pet should win Best in Show. They ask Minnie for help.

"All our pets are the best," says Minnie with a smile. "So they all win!"

Pete brings the grand prize to the stage. "Pet treats for everyone," he hollers. "Come and get it!"

Hot dog!

Donald's Stinky Day

It's another beautiful day in Hot Dog Hills. Donald is taking a leisurely drive through the park.

Suddenly, he sees Butch run by, dragging Pete behind him. "What's he so excited about?" Donald wonders out loud. Butch starts barking at a fuzzy tail in a tree.

"Aw, it's a kitty," says Donald. "Don't worry, I'll get you down," he calls to the creature.

Donald climbs the tree and points to his hat. "Hop on!"

A moment later, Pete laughs and laughs when he sees what is sitting on Donald's head. "That ain't no kitty!"

Butch lunges at the animal, who turns around, lifts her tail, and sprays a smelly cloud in Butch's face. Donald saved a skunk!

Donald hops into his Cabin Cruiser and heads to Mickey's Garage, where he finds Goofy working on his Turbo Tubster. Goofy takes one whiff and turns on the shower. "I think you and your friend might need some Tubster time," he says.

"My friend?" asks Donald. He looks down. "*Wak!* Get outta here!"

All Donald wants to do is work on his roadster, but the skunk won't leave his side. She picks up a wrench.

"Aww, she's trying to help you," says Goofy.

"I don't need her help!" Donald shouts.

Uh-oh! She accidentally drops the wrench on Donald's foot.

"YEOW!"

Mickey and Minnie come in to see what the commotion is about.

"She really likes you!" Minnie says.

"Still, it's an odd choice for a pet," says Mickey.

"SHE'S NOT MY PET!" Donald hollers.

Donald's buddies send him through the Auto Wash so he can be de-stink-ified. First comes the soapy water—*whoosh!* Then the brushes—scrub-a-dub!

"You're as fresh as a daisy!" Minnie says with a giggle.

To cheer Donald up, Goofy invites him to lunch, and Mickey offers to take him fishing after that.

"Sounds great!" says Donald. "As long as that smelly skunk doesn't come with us."

Donald looks around but doesn't see the skunk anywhere. He and Goofy jump into the Cabin Cruiser and drive to the restaurant.

Donald and Goofy
order two special
double-diggity dogs
with mustard,
pickles, and tofu.
"My favorite!" says
Donald. "All it needs
is ketchup."

Look who came to
help her best buddy, Donald!

Donald puts his hands on
his hips and glares at the smelly skunk.

"You are exasperating! Now give me that ketchup." He angrily
grabs the bottle and squeezes it. SPLAT!

"That's it!" says Donald. "I'm going fishing!

Mickey meets Donald at Hot Dog Lake. Soon the two friends are happily fishing off the Cabin Cruiser.

"Wow, it's amazing to see you relax so fast, Donald," Mickey says. "What's your secret?"

"I made this a No Skunks zone," Donald answers proudly.

But Donald is not relaxed for very long. The skunk pops out of her hiding spot once again.

Donald flies out of his seat . . .

the skunk falls into the lake . . .

and the fish leap out of the water to escape the stink.

"We hit the jackpot!" Mickey laughs. "Thanks to that clever cutie."

But once the skunk jumps back onto the boat, the fish jump back into the lake.

"Easy, Donald," Mickey says cheerfully. "She's just trying to be a helpful friend."

"Friend, huh?" Donald huffs. Then he gets an idea.

There's nothing better than a picnic with a pal! Donald takes the skunk back to the park.

"Oh, no!" he says slyly. "I forgot the potato chips. Be right back!"

"Bye-bye, stinker!" Donald calls from his roadster. "Have fun in the park . . . far away from me!"

He zips down the road and accidentally bumps into a beehive. He turns around to see a swarm of angry bees chasing him!

"*Waak!*" Donald squawks. "What do they want?"

Donald steps on the gas to escape the bees. He zigzags around cars and zooms up the hill toward Mickey's Garage.

Donald skids to a stop and jumps out of the roadster. Everyone panics at the sight of the buzzing swarm of bees.

Mickey and Minnie hide under a barrel. Goofy dives into his Turbo Tubster. But the bees only want Donald. He crashes into a pile of cans while trying to run away.

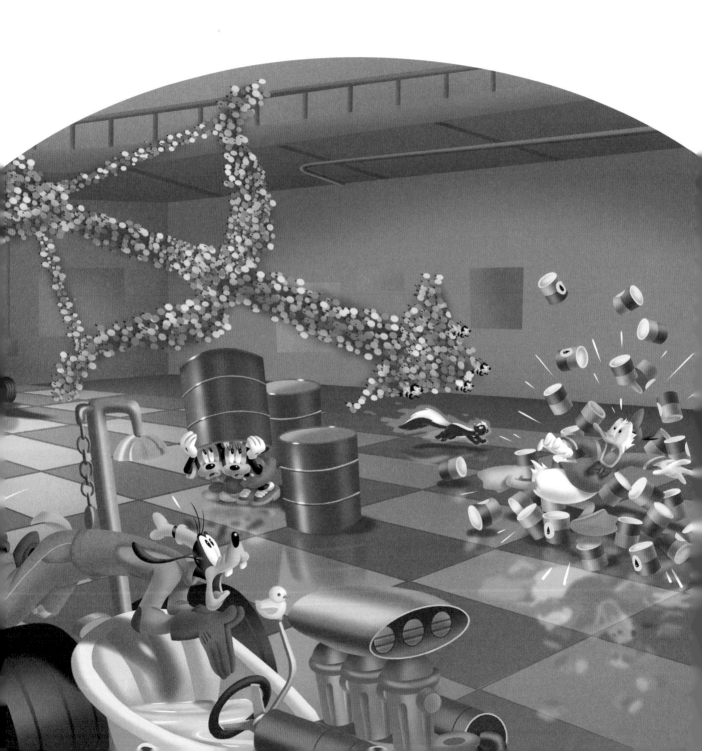

Just as the bees are about to sting Donald, the skunk appears! She lifts her tail and blasts them with a huge cloud of smelliness. The bees stop, turn around, and buzz off!

Donald gives the skunk a big hug. "You saved me! I can't believe it!"

"Believe it," says Minnie. "That's what friends do."

"Friends," says Donald warmly. "That's right!"

The skunk licks her new friend's face. "Aww, cut that out," Donald says, chuckling.

Donald and his new friend go back to the park to help Daisy with her daisies.

Donald takes a big sniff. "*Bee*-utiful!"

Look Before You Leap!

Mickey and Goofy are enjoying a quiet game of chess. Just as Mickey is about to make a move, something soars through the window and lands right in the middle of the chessboard.

"What was that?" Mickey asks. The two friends look carefully at something that looks right back at them.

It is green. It has webbed feet. It says, *"Ribbit, ribbit."*

It is a frog—a very jumpy frog. Goofy tries to grab it. Plop! The frog leaps out of Goofy's hands and right toward the . . .

. . . kitchen sink. *Kerplunk!* Water splashes all over the kitchen floor.

"You really should look before you leap!" Mickey says to the frog.

"What are we going to do about this big puddle?" Goofy asks.

"Oh, Toodles!" Mickey calls. "We need some Mouseketools—right now!"

Toodles brings three tools: a mop, a hot-air balloon, and a rowboat. Which one does Mickey need to clean up the kitchen?

"The mop is the right tool for this job," says Mickey. "Thanks, Toodles!" He and Goofy mop up the water from the floor.

"Gawrsh," says Goofy, "all this hard work is making me hungry." He decides to make lunch: a super-duper stacked sandwich with everything on it. "Yummers!"

Goofy is just about to take a big bite when the frog takes a giant leap and . . .

Squish!

"Stop!" Mickey cries. "You're about to get a frog in your throat!"

"You really should look before you leap," Goofy says to the frog, "and I should look before I eat! What should we do with this jumpy little fella?"

"I think we should find a nice pond," Mickey replies. "Then he can leap without causing any trouble."

Goofy carries the frog outside. It is a beautiful sunny day. Daisy is doing an art project in the Clubhouse backyard.

"Hold on tight to our frog friend," Mickey says. "He's pretty slippery."

"I have him," says Goofy.

The frog wriggles a little.

"I have him," says Goofy.

The frog slips and slides.

"*Oops!* I don't have him!" Goofy yelps as the frog leaps right toward . . .

Daisy's painting! Splat! The frog lands on
her paint palette, sending different colors of
paint flying in all directions.

"You should look before you leap!" Daisy
says to the frog. "Now my painting—and my
clothes—are a mess."

But the frog keeps jumping, leaving a trail of
yellow webbed footprints.

"Hey, little friend," Mickey says to the frog, "slow down!" But it is too late. The frog leaps out from behind Daisy's painting and heads straight toward . . .

Mickey's bicycle. Boing! The frog zooms down the road, holding tightly to the handlebars. He is headed straight for a cliff.

"Oh, no!" Goofy shouts.

"Oh, Toodles!" yells Mickey. "We need you!"

Toodles brings three new tools: a lasso, a shovel, and a flashlight. Which one does Mickey need to rescue the frog?

"The lasso is the right tool for this job," says Mickey. "Thanks, Toodles!"

Mickey and Goofy carefully pull the bicycle back from the edge of the cliff.

The frog lands on the soft grass, looks up at them, and lets out a *"Ribbit."*

"We need to find somewhere safe for this little guy," Goofy says. "He keeps leaping toward trouble."

Before they can get their hands on him, the frog hops away down the road with Mickey and Goofy following fast behind him.

The frog stops hopping right in front of the Hot Dog Hills pizzeria.

Slowly, Mickey and Goofy creep up behind him, hoping he doesn't

notice.

"We've got to get him before he leaps!" Mickey whispers.

They walk on tiptoe, trying not to make a sound. Slowly, quietly,

Mickey reaches out an arm—and right then the frog leaps onto a . . .

. . . pizza pie. Slosh! Tomato sauce splatters and sprays all over.

The chef is not happy with the new pizza topping. "You should look before you leap!" shouts the man behind the counter.

The frog stops for a moment to clean himself off. Before Mickey and Goofy catch up to him, he hops down Main Street, headed right toward Minnie and Pluto.

Mickey and Goofy are tired and nearly out of breath from this wild, wacky frog chase.

"Maybe Minnie and Pluto can help us catch our frog friend," says Mickey.

"And take him to a nice pond," Goofy adds.

But the frog has other ideas. He takes a great big leap and lands right inside . . .

. . . Minnie's goldfish bowl. Splash!

The big wave makes the goldfish fly right out. Minnie gently puts the goldfish back into its bowl. "I don't know if we'll ever find a pond for froggie. We need some help!" Goofy says with a sigh.

"Oh, Toodles!" Mickey calls.

Toodles brings three new tools: a birthday cake, a beach ball, and a net. Which one will help catch the frog?

"The net is the right tool for this job," says Mickey. "Thanks, Toodles!"

With a swing and a swoosh, Mickey scoops the frog up into the net. He is safe but not happy.

"He seems sad," Goofy says.

"I think you're right, Goofy," Mickey agrees. Then he looks ahead and sees something that makes him—and the frog—smile. "I think we've found just the right place for you, froggie," Mickey says.

Mickey walks quickly down the street, careful not to disturb the frog too much. A few moments later, he gently lifts the frog out of the net, ready to show him his new home.

"I think you'll like this spot," Mickey tells him. "It has plenty of cold water for swimming, and a great view of Main Street. Ready to see your new—"

But the frog is impatient. He slips out of Mickey's hands and leaps straight for the . . .

. . . fountain. He lands with a splash right next to another frog.

"*Ribbit, ribbit,*" he says.

"*Ribbit, ribbit,*" she replies.

"We did it!" says Goofy. "We finally found somewhere that he likes enough to stick around instead of leaping away."

"It may not be a pond," says Mickey, "but it's a great place for him to splash and leap."

"And look!" Minnie adds. "Your new friend found a new friend of his own."

They watch the frogs swim happily around the fountain.

Suddenly, a goldfish jumps out of the water! Minnie's goldfish is excited to see another fish.

Minnie looks at the small goldfish bowl compared to the big fountain and the animals that live there. It seems like the perfect spot for her goldfish, too. She decides to let the goldfish go but promises to visit.

Mickey, Goofy, Minnie, and Pluto walk back down Main Street, past the pizzeria, past the cliff, and back to the Clubhouse. This time there is no chasing and no leaping.

"I'm in the mood for pizza!" Minnie says. Donald and Daisy agree to help her cook and bake a fresh pizza from scratch.

"Yummers!" says Goofy. "But Mickey and I have one quick thing to finish first."

Mickey and Goofy get back to their game of chess. Mickey stares at the board, trying to decide his next move.

"C'mon, Mickey," Goofy says. "You haven't made a move in a long time."

"I know. I know," replies Mickey. "I just want to make sure I look carefully before I leap!"

A Goofy Fairy Tale

Tonight is Story Night in the Clubhouse Library. Mickey is going to read a bedtime story.

"Aw, shucks," says Goofy. "I thought it was Magic Night."

"How will we decide which story to read?" Minnie asks.

"I'll use magic to pick a book," says Goofy. "Book-a-doodle-doo. Fly away and shoo!"

Oh, no! Goofy uses the wrong magic words. All the stories disappear!

Mickey asks Professor Von Drake if he knows where the stories went. "They're in a gold storybook in the Land of Fairy Tales," says the professor.

Outside, the professor opens a magic door to the Land of Fairy Tales. "The gold storybook is in the Castle of the Beast," he says. "It has three shapes on its cover—a heart, a diamond, and a rose."

Oops! Goofy slips and falls through the magic door. A wall of glass slams shut!

"Hoo-boy," says the professor. "My remote control went kaput. Goofy's stuck."

"Oh, dear," Daisy says. "Goofy can't get the gold storybook by himself."

"He'll just goof up," adds Donald.

"I'm sure you can do it, pal," Mickey tells Goofy. "Good luck!"

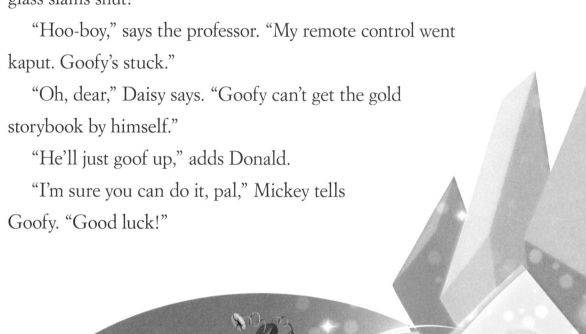

Dressed in his new fairy tale clothes,
Goofy starts down a path.

"Gawrsh," says Goofy. "Which
way leads to the beast's castle?"

"Go right!" answers someone
with a tiny voice.

Goofy is so surprised he falls to the ground.

"You're a goofy fella!" says a small knight.

"Goofyfella!" Goofy says, laughing. "That'll be my fairy tale name."

"We're Chip and Dale Thumb," Chip Thumb, the small knight, says.

"But we've got to go," adds Dale Thumb. "Big problem at the
castle!"

"Okay," says Goofyfella. "See ya!"

Soon Goofyfella comes upon Pied Piper Donald and Pluto the Merry Dog. They're trying to lead ducklings to a pond.

"They won't follow me!" says Pied Piper Donald.

Goofyfella tries to teach Pied Piper Donald a new song. But he drops the flute, and it breaks.

"Sorry," he says. "Oh, Toodles!"

Toodles's cousin, Goofles, comes to help with four Mouseketools— suction cups, sticky tape, an oar, and a Mystery Mouseketool. Goofyfella chooses the tape to fix the flute. It works!

When Pied Piper Donald plays the new song, the ducklings line up and follow him. "Thanks!" he says.

Deep in the woods, Goofyfella gets lost and runs into Hansel and Gretel Mouse. They're lost, too.

"Maybe somebody in that house can help us," says Goofyfella.

"No. That's the witch's house!" Gretel Mouse warns.

Just then someone calls, "Hello-o-o!" It's Witch Clarabelle!

"Are you a good witch?" asks Goofyfella.

"Oh, yes," says Witch Clarabelle, laughing.

"I'm not scary at all."

Witch Clarabelle is making a big batch of Merry Muffins, but she can't find her mixing spoon.

Goofyfella calls for Goofles and chooses the oar.

"It's moo-arvelous!" says Witch Clarabelle.

Goofyfella accidentally knocks a basket of berries right into the batter! "Gawrsh," he says. "I'm such a goof."

"No! That's just what my batter needs," says Witch Clarabelle.

"I like being helpful," says Goofyfella. "But I need to get to the castle."

"Just follow the diamond shapes," says Witch Clarabelle.

Goofyfella says goodbye and hurries on his way.

The diamond shapes lead Goofyfella to a hill made of crystal. At the top is the beast's castle. "It's kinda scary-looking," says Goofyfella. "But I'm not afraid. I'm going to climb up there and get the gold storybook."

The hill is super slippery. "Whoopsie! Looks like I need a Mouseketool," says Goofyfella. "Oh, Goofles!"

Goofles has two Mouseketools left—the suction cups and the Mystery Mouseketool.

Goofyfella chooses the suction cups. He puts them on his shoes and marches right up the hill.

Goofyfella sees Chip and Dale Thumb at the castle door.

"We've come to rescue Daisy Beauty," Dale Thumb tells him.

Goofy rings the gigantic castle doorbell.

Beast Pete comes to the door. "What do you want?" he roars.

"We want you to let Daisy Beauty go!" says Chip Thumb.

"It's not nice to keep her locked inside," says Goofyfella.

"I know," Beast Pete admits. "I just wanted a friend."

"Well, let's have a party," Goofyfella says. "That's a good way to make friends."

Beast Pete is delighted. "There will be music and dancing," he says. "And I'll invite everyone to come!" Beast Pete turns to Daisy Beauty. "Will you be my guest?" he asks politely.

Daisy Beauty sees that Beast Pete is really very kind.

"Yes," she answers. "We can be friends, too."

All of a sudden, Beast Pete turns into a prince. Daisy Beauty's friendship broke the spell!

Everyone enjoys the party—especially Prince Pete!

"I owe this all to you, Goofyfella," he says.

"How can I repay you?"

"I'm looking for the gold storybook," Goofyfella says.

"If the book is in my library," says Prince Pete,

"it's yours."

Prince Pete's library is stacked high with books.

"What does the gold storybook look like?" he asks.

"It's decorated with a heart, a diamond, and a rose," says Goofyfella.

"I see it!" shouts Daisy Beauty. "But it's up so high."

"I know just what to do," says Goofyfella. "Oh, Goofles!"

The Mystery Mouseketool is a bunch of balloons!
Goofyfella uses them to float up to the top shelf and
grab the gold storybook.

"I've got it!" shouts Goofyfella. "But how am I
going to get down?"

Chip and Dale Thumb come to the rescue, popping the balloons one at a time.

Goofyfella safely drifts back to the ground.

"Great job!" says Prince Pete.

It's time for
Goofyfella to go
home. Prince Pete
asks Rosalie the
dragon to give him
a ride. Goofyfella
holds the gold
storybook tight and
waves goodbye to his new
friends. *"Wa-ha-ha-hooey!"*

At the Clubhouse, the professor gets the
remote control working. Goofy jumps right through the open door.

Mickey opens the gold storybook, and the missing stories fly back
into their books!

"So, what story are we gonna
hear?" Goofy asks.

"Your story!" Daisy
says. "How'd you find
the book?"

"Well," begins
Goofy, "I guess
you could say
I found it in
my own goofy
way. . . ."

Campy Camper Day

One morning in Hot Dog Hills, Mickey is working on something special to take his friends on a camping trip.

"Whatcha got there, Mickey?" Goofy asks.

Mickey pulls off the sheet covering his creation. "Let me present the ultimate Campy Camper! It can pop out tents, launch rubber rafts, hand out fishing rods, and set up its very own campfire!" he says proudly. "It even has room for as many hot dogs as you can pack!"

"Terrif!" says Goofy. "Back in a jiff!"

Goofy returns a moment later and starts packing. "This camper is hot dog heaven!"

Just then Mickey's electronic fishing game vibrates and plays a tune. "Oh, boy! A new tournament is starting," he says to himself. While Goofy's back is turned, Mickey sneaks away to play his game.

"All done packing and ready to go, Mickey," Goofy says—but Mickey isn't there. "Hey, where did he go?"

Minnie is ready to go, too. But she can't find Donald and Daisy.
Minnie hears a lot of noise coming from the break room and goes to
investigate.

Mickey can't stop playing his fishing game. *BEEP! BUZZ!*

Donald is watching a show. "And now back to the adventures of . . ."

Daisy is listening to a podcast. "It was midnight when the detectives
arrived on the scene. . . ."

"I see you're all having fun, but we're getting ready to go camping,
remember?" Minnie says to her friends. "Let's put away the screens and
just enjoy our time outdoors with each other."

Mickey climbs behind the wheel of the Campy Camper, and the gang is on their way. They pass rolling hills, winding rivers, and a field of wildflowers. But Daisy and Donald miss it all. Their eyes are glued to their screens!

The friends soon arrive at the campground.

"Guess we'd better start settin' up tents," says Goofy.

"No need, pal," says Mickey. "Step back and let my Campy Camper do it all!"

Mickey presses a button, and five tents shoot out of the camper.

"Wow!" Minnie says. "You thought of everything, Mickey!" She turns around, but no one is there. "Mickey?"

Mickey, Donald, and Daisy are staring at their electronic gadgets again.

Minnie can't believe her friends are still obsessed with their screens. "Just look at the beauty around you!" she says.

"Like them fishies jumpin' in a crystal-clear lake," Goofy adds.

The gang decides to go fishing together—real fishing, not video game fishing.

Everyone lines up at the Campy Camper. Mickey pushes a button, and with a whoosh and a whir, a mechanical hand appears. One by one, they all get the fishing gear they need.

Goofy leads the way to a lovely fishing spot at the edge of the lake. An eagle circles overhead.

"Hiya, baldy!" Goofy shouts. The bird replies with a screech.

Minnie is delighted. "Isn't this wonderful?" she asks.

Buzz! Mickey's video game vibrates in his pocket. "Hot dog, daily reward!" he whispers. He can't resist the game, so he hides in the bushes to play for bonus points.

Donald tips his fishing rod back over his shoulder, then yanks it
forward to cast the line into the lake. But the hook gets caught on
something.

Donald pulls and pulls. "Say, what's the big idea?" he squawks.

Donald pulls harder. The fishing line comes free and sails out over the lake, and on the hook is Mickey's video game! The gadget catches the eye of the hungry eagle, who grabs it with his talons, thinking it's a real fish.

Donald holds tight to his fishing pole. The eagle drags him back and forth across the water, making gigantic waves.

The eagle tries to take a bite out of the game, but it zaps him and he lets it go. It tumbles through the air and bops Mickey on the head. A moment later, Donald crashes into Mickey.

Minnie picks up the game and hands it to Mickey. "I know you like your game," she says sweetly, "but since we're here, let's enjoy the outdoors together."

Mickey apologizes and agrees.

Next everyone decides to go for a hike in the woods.

Before long, Daisy gets an alert on her phone. Her favorite podcast has posted a new episode. Daisy just has to listen right away. She puts in her earbuds and starts walking backward so no one will see what she is doing.

Daisy is too focused on her podcast to pay attention to where she's going. She tumbles down a slope and lands in the bushes! Everybody helps Daisy back onto the trail.

Minnie finds Daisy's phone on the ground and hands it to her.

These little screens are causing big problems!

When the gang returns to the campsite, Minnie has another idea. "Let's all go rafting," she says.

With the press of a button, the Campy Camper produces an inflatable raft and four paddles. When they are in the water, Donald sits in the back of the raft and shouts out directions.

But while his pals are looking at the river, Donald is watching a show on his tablet. The friends paddle wildly in the fast-moving water and don't notice that they are heading toward a waterfall! The raft lands safely, but everyone loses their paddles. They are stranded.

Goofy spots the eagle. "Hey, baldy!" he shouts. "Can you lend us a wing?"

The eagle swoops down to shore and lands on the Campy Camper. He leans in an open window and screeches a message.

"Translating bald eagle," the camper says in a robotic voice. "Mickey and gang in trouble. Camper rescue mode engaged."

The Campy Camper powers itself up and flies to the river. It uses sonar to find one of the lost paddles and tosses the paddle to Goofy. Everyone cheers! The camper winks a headlight and flies back to the campsite.

When they are safely on shore, Donald apologizes for not paying attention. Mickey and Daisy are sorry, too.

"Aw, shucks," says Goofy. "The day's not over yet!"

After the sun goes down, everyone gathers around the campfire for hot dogs and marshmallows.

"It's so nice to just unplug and spend time with friends," says Mickey.

The night sky twinkles above. "Oh!" exclaims Minnie. "I see a shooting star! Everyone make a wish."

"I wish we could camp out like this every year," says Daisy.

Her pals agree.